The POOPicorn

Hilary Whiton

Illustrated by
Stephen Stone

Cozmo was good at one thing.

He could sniff out the freshest, smelliest, most delicious poop on the prairie.

That's what dung beetles do!

The problem was that as good as he was at finding the poop, he was terrible at landing on it. When he spotted a bison herd and smelled fresh dung, Cozmo went through his landing checklist.

"Feet untucked, check."

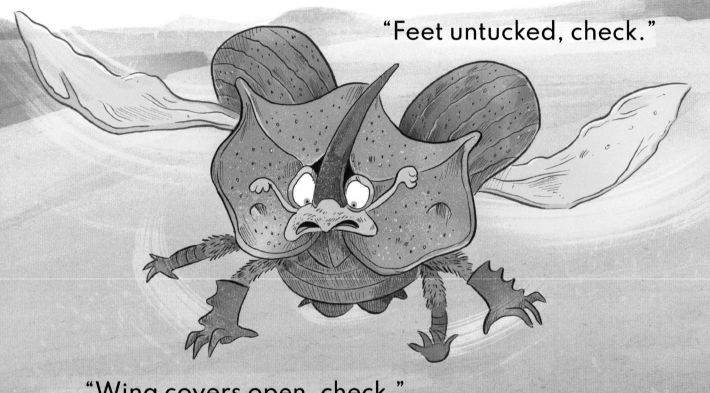

"Wing covers open, check."

"Slow down…..,"

Cozmo perched on the bison's snout and looked into her surprised eyes.

"Whoa," she exclaimed. "Are you a unicorn?"

"A unicorn?" Cozmo asked.

"You know, the magical creature with a horn on its head! Are you one?" she asked again.

Before Cozmo could answer, the bison snapped her head to bite at a fly. Cozmo had to hold on tight with all six of his legs!

"Sorry, Unicorn!" the young bison said.
"These flies are always bugging me, biting me, and buzzing around me. I wish they would just go away!"

"Well, little lady, I may be able to help you with your fly problem, but first I have to fix my landing problem," Cozmo said, lifting off again.

When he smelled another excellent pile of poop,
Cozmo went through his landing checklist again.

"Feet untucked, check."

"Wing covers open, check."

"Slow down……,"

Cozmo got to his legs and brushed off some grass. It was yellow and dry. Over in the cow pasture, where his dung beetle family was from, the grass was soft and green.

Cozmo knew he could help make this grass green too, if only he could land on a poop patty.

He lifted off again. And determined to land this time, he went through a different checklist.

"Feet untucked, nope."

"Wing covers open, nope."

"Speed up…..,"

He was right on top of a poop patty!

That's when he realized that crashing wasn't

his problem, it was his speciality!

Cozmo took a big **SLUUUUUURP** of poop, and then stuck his horn down into the patty and began to dig with his legs.

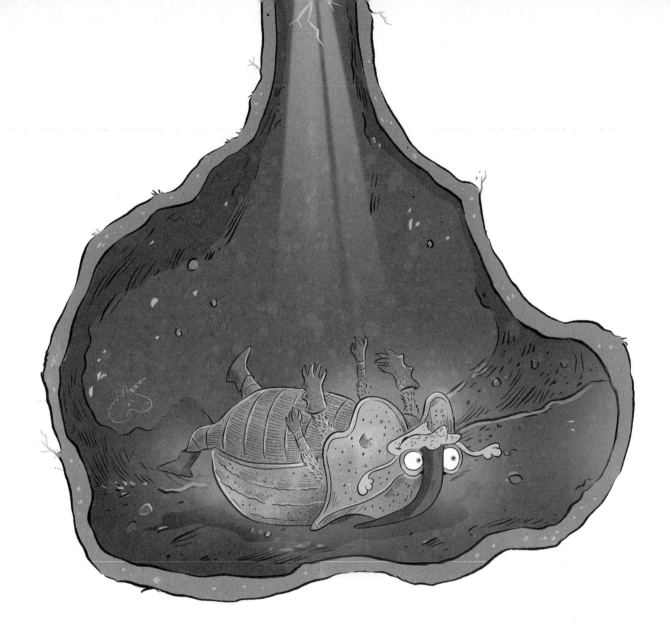

But he didn't get too far before ... **PLOP!**

Cozmo fell down a tunnel and landed on his back.

That's when he saw the most beautiful hornless dung beetle in the world.

"Hi!" she said. "I'm Rose."

"Hi," Cozmo said, flipping over onto his legs again. "I'm Clumsy, I mean Cozmo!"

"I can see that," Rose said, laughing.

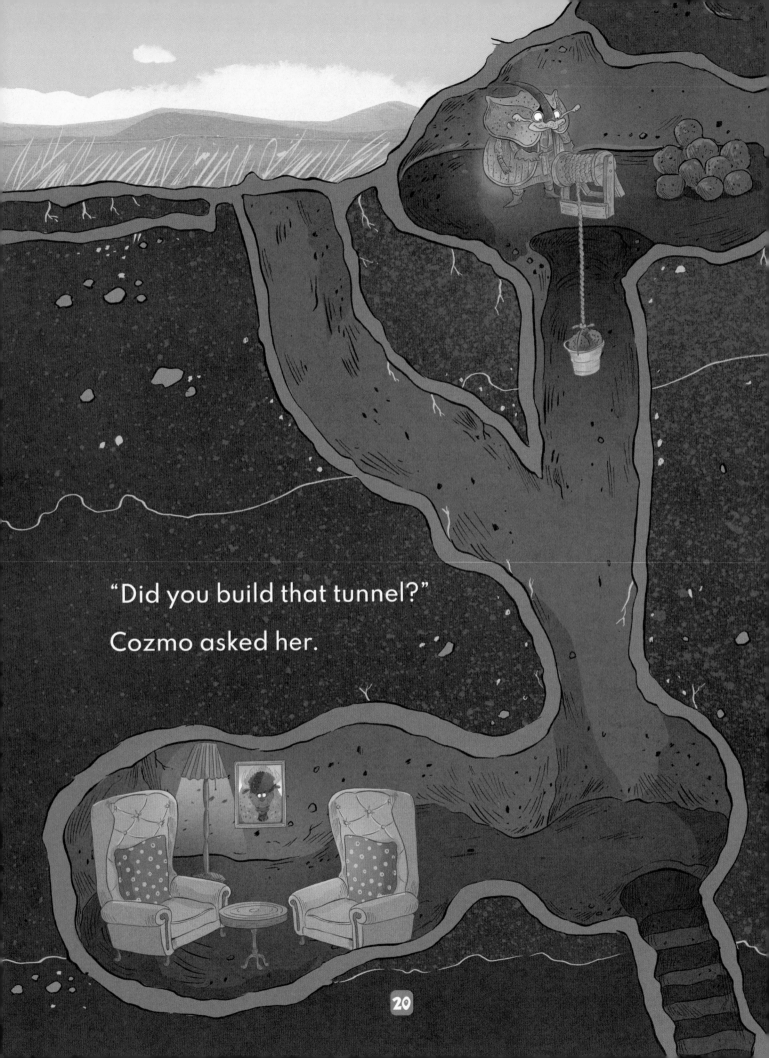

"Did you build that tunnel?"

Cozmo asked her.

"Yep!" said Rose. "Dug it myself.

Wanna help me with the poop?"

"Okay," Cozmo said.

Cozmo liked Rose. She taught him her mother's recipe for poo ball tea cakes! They rolled the poop into bite-sized nuggets and then sprinkled them with dirt to keep them fresh.

They piled them up and Rose said they would be good to eat on a day they couldn't find fresh poop.

Then Cozmo told Rose about crashing into the little bison.

"She thought I was a unicorn," he laughed. "Because of my horn."

"Ha ha," chuckled Rose and then she said,

" We are kinda magical creatures, though."

"We are?" questioned Cozmo.

"Yeah, can you imagine the plains without us?" asked Rose.

"It would be pretty poopy!" Cozmo said.

"Yep. And taking all that poop underground helps the flies go away," explained Rose.

"The bison will be happy about that!" said Cozmo.

"The poop helps the grass grow too," Rose said.

"It's too dirty a job for any old unicorn,"

Cozmo said.

Then he thought of something and smiled.

Later that day, Rose made a big ball of poop.
Cozmo helped her gather poop into the tunnel
little by little and then they covered it with soil.

"This will be perfect!" Rose said.

"Perfect for what?" asked Cozmo.

"For this." And Rose climbed on top of the big
ball and laid an egg!

Soon there would be a dung beetle larva to help the prairie become a beautiful place.

"Maybe we should call him **POOPicorn!**" Cozmo said, winking.

As Cozmo and Rose's larva grew beneath the prairie, the young bison and her mother grazed on the newly sprouted grass.

"The prairie grass is so soft and green. And the flies are gone," the bison mother marveled.

The little bison nodded in agreement and then leaned down to a poop patty and called,

"Thank you, Unicorn!"

For the Recipe

Poo Ball
Tea CAKES
for Humans

Visit - www.poopicorn.com

Q. & A with **Dr. Frank Krell**
Senior Curator of Entomology, Department of Zoology, Denver Museum of Nature & Science

How many bison roamed the Great Plains 200 years ago?
About 50-60 million.

Did they poop a lot?
Each one pooped about ten times a day. That's a lot of poop!

When you pick up bison poop to look for dung beetles, are you protected by a fence?
No, I have to be really careful, because bison can be aggressive. I always have a team member watch the herd while I collect samples. Otherwise, I might have my head down and not notice them getting near. When they get close, I have to get into my car for protection. Sometimes the bison will play with my sample buckets, which is really annoying. One time, they licked my car mirrors. I had to go through the car wash several times to get the lick marks off, because their saliva is really sticky!

Can anyone collect dung beetles?
Yes, but do not stick your fingers in poop and do not get close to cattle or bison! Collect fresh dung patties with a shovel and put them in a bucket. Take the bucket home and fill it with water. Dung beetles are lighter than water, so they will float up and the poop will sink down. You can also pick dung beetles out of poop with forceps, which are like big tweezers. Pro Tip: Always carry hand wipes when you are hunting for dung beetles.

Do Rainbow Scarab Beetles, like Cozmo, really have a good sense of smell?
Yes, they do. They find their food and mates by scent. Rainbow Scarab Beetles smell with their antennae. The yellow pom-poms at the end of their antennae bear well over 1000 sensilla. The sensilla are tiny organs that sense smelly stuff. They can sniff out poop from far away. They think poop smells delicious!

Are Rainbow Scarab Beetles good flyers and clumsy landers like Cozmo?
Yes, they are surprisingly good flyers. You would not expect cannonball shaped insects with two little wings to fly well, but they do. They take off quickly and are fast fliers. But when they land, they just tumble. They have heavy bodies and thick legs which are good for digging, but are not good for landing.

Cozmo and Rose made tunnels underground. Do Rainbow Scarab Beetles really do that?

Yes, mostly the females make tunnels underground. The tunnels provide protection for the eggs, larva, and adult beetles. If Rainbow Scarabs laid their eggs directly on poop patties, predators like birds, lizards, and toads could easily eat the larvae.

Do dung beetles really improve the health of the grasslands?

Poop can be fertilizer for grass and plants, but the nutrients need to get to the roots of plants. Dung beetles bring poop underground and mix it with soil, bringing the nutrients where the plants need them. Dung Beetles are also helpful in reducing the fly population by removing poop that flies like to lay their eggs in, and by disrupting fly maggots in poop patties as they dig through.

Why do the males have horns and how do they use them?

The most important role of the male Rainbow Scarab Beetle, apart from mating, is to protect its nest. They often use their big shield (pronotum) to block the nest tunnel, which stops other beetles from getting in. They will also use their horns to fight off other males if needed.

How long do Rainbow Scarab Beetles live?

After a Rainbow Scarab egg hatches into a larva, it lives underground and eats poop for 6-12 months. It eats and eats until it is so fat that its skin can't stretch any further. Then in molts (sheds it's skin), and again eats and eats until it is so fat that its skin is tight and it molts again. Then it eats until it is fat a third time and finally it molts into a pupa. The pupa hatches into an adult. Adult beetles don't live very long. Their body is designed to live just long enough to mate. So, a Rainbow Scarab beetle is a larva longer than it is an adult. The larvae eat much more than the adult beetles. The larvae have strong mandibles (jaws) and can chew through poop. The adults can only drink up the soupy part of the poop.

When and why did you develop your interest in beetles?

When I was ten years old I wanted to collect sea shells, but I did not live near a beach. So, I had to collect something else and beetles are similar to shells. They are hard, beautiful, unique, and they come in different colors and fascinating shapes. I started collecting them in 1976 and I have never stopped.

Resource:
F. Krell, personal communication, December 5, 2020.

To my parents, Jane and Bill, who showed me the wonders of the world
H.W.

In memory of my father and mother, Fred and Mary
S.S.

Hilary Whiton (Author)

Hilary grew up in Boulder, Colorado and earned her B.A. and teaching credential from the University of San Diego. She has taught kindergarten through second grade and worked as a literacy interventionist. A proud Coloradan and outdoor enthusiast, Hilary is passionate about preserving nature by educating children about the importance of all creatures. She currently lives in Louisville, Colorado with her husband, three children and two dogs.
www.hilarywhiton.com

Stephen Stone (Designer & Illustrator)

Stephen lives in Derbyshire, England with his wife and slightly aloof orange cat Vincent van Mog. He began his creative career training to be a fashion designer before becoming a university lecturer. Now retired from teaching he works as a professional freelance designer and illustrator. Stephen has published books with many mainstream publishers and indie authors. He has a passion for developing expressive and animated characters, especially the four and six legged kind!
www.yellowstonestudio.co.uk

Text copyright © 2021 by Hilary Whiton
Illustrations copyright © Stephen Stone

Published by Hilary Whiton
www.hilarywhiton.com

Library of Congress Cataloging -in Publication-Data
Names: Whiton, Hilary - Author / Stone, Stephen - Illustrator
Title: The Poopicorn ,Hilary Whiton, illustrated by Stephen Stone
ISBN 978-1-7365927-0-0 (hbk)
ISBN 978-1-7365927-1-7 (pbk)

Display type set in Aklatanic TSO by Tomasz Dudziak
Text type set in Spartan (Google Font) originally designed by Matt Bailey
Designed by Stephen Stone

Spot the Unicorn
Pages: 9,12,18,21,23,27,31,33

Made in the USA
Monee, IL
01 July 2021